T0368430

My world in short stories

Piedad Romero-Torres

With Gratitude,

This book is dedicated to all of my students, the children and adults, that at one point were part of my life and enhanced my purpose as an educator! Thank you to my children, and husband for your constant support. You are my real story.

General Coordination: Laura Cajamarca Bravo
Illustrations: Daniela Torres
Design and layout of the book: Camila Laverde

INDEX

FOREWORD

I have encountered some of my former students in different ways. Some I met again while I was eating in a restaurant, in a hospital or just walking in the streets. Many did achieve their dreams; others are still working on them. The one that shocked me the most was when I crossed paths with a young man who came towards me asking me, "is that you Ms. Torres?" I was shocked and frightened with his effusive hug. "I am that kid that used to sit on the last row of room 202," he said. "You used to talk to me about believing in myself but that I had to work for my dreams, to finish school. I did it Ms.!"

I enlisted in the Marines and now I am working towards a degree. He claimed that while I was telling a story he used to imagine himself going over the same emotions. Those moments made him self-reflect and helped him improve.

Another meeting happened while I was picking up clothes from the cleaners. A young lady smiled at me and asked me if my last name was Torres. "How do you know?" I asked. "You changed my life Ms. Torres! Let me introduce you to my daughter," she said. Then, I recognized her. She had attended one of my GED night courses. If you ever need me, I am here for you," she said.

"This is my last year as a medical resident." I felt my face redden. "Yes Ms.! I just followed your advice." I asked her out loud. "What did I say to you?" "Your stories were my guide," she said. "I learned to trust my inner thoughts and believe in myself as an individual."

There are many other encounters but to tell them all will be like writing another book. I have learned that these stories have enlightened, strengthened or changed the way people lived or saw life. My hope for many is to learn how to read between the lines and to believe in the magic of writing, to create short stories with endings to their liking and stories that brighten their souls.

7

Door

Life changes.

Knock, knock, knock! The bell rings, I couldn't see what was happening. My brother got to the door before me. Suddenly, I see my grandmother and Nana opening the door. My Nana started screaming happily. I heard my brother running back towards the kitchen. I was so confused, a lady had just arrived, my brother said. She was carrying several bags of luggage, and started coming towards me. My grandmother screamed and said "It's your mother, come and greet her."

Oh! It was my mother! She had come back! Everything was so confusing; my tia Gigi wasn't greeting or speaking to my mom. My abuela seemed worried. My tia Alma was happy, but at the same time was sad. Nana was also sad but happy too. She was always telling us "Now your life is going to change, be happy, but don't forget me." I didn't understand all the commotion. To my understanding, my life had changed a long time ago when my mom had left us with abuelita to go to the USA.

Tia Gigi was my favorite aunt; she was always happy and liked to talk to us kids. (Why was my mom so upset at her?) She used to take us to different places to play. She had three kids, our cousins that we played with all the time.

She was no chef, but used to bake and cater other people's parties. She also used to teach in a small school.

Tia Alma was always working so she was never home, but used to tell us to study (she checked our notebooks and book bags at night.) She used to say that whatever we read, studied/learned/observed/investigated were the solid base of our education. Tia Alma always reinforced that "Education is the one thing no one will ever take away from you." No one will ever take you for a fool.

Abuelita was the disciplinarian always making sure that we didn't do the wrong thing. She was an authoritarian soul, very steeped in our family heritage. She used to tell us, "Remember, your grandfather was Italian!"

Luz was our Nana, she took care of all of us (cousins and all the kids,, she fed us, dressed us, made sure we were well taken care of. She had three kids of her own, but they were much older. It seemed like her life had been harsh. She defended us when we were in trouble, and saved food for anyone who felt hungry late in the afternoon, or made a sopita.

They all (the grown-ups) seemed to hide something. They murmured around us and every time we got close to them, they'd get quiet and tell us to leave.

Soon enough, I would learn the truth.

10

11

Seahorse

First Move—towards the truth!

It was late afternoon when I realized something was happening in the living room. My mother was screaming. Luz was making sure we got upstairs, that we wouldn't come down to the living room at all.

She had left a live seahorse in front of the refrigerator door, since I've always been afraid of small animals; she knew I wouldn't come down. Instead, I climbed on to the balcony to watch and, to my surprise, saw Luz was laughing, and my mom was furious. My father was going back and forth looking for something.

He was desperate! My mom was screaming, "the red car had been vandalized and both doors were missing!!!" Years later I learned that my father knew about it, but hid it from my mom to avoid a confrontation. However, that was the anchor that made my mom decide it was time to go someplace far away to start a new life with her husband. My father was offered a position at the Automaker Corporation, but needed to go to the USA to learn about injector pumps and engine turbos to use them in our country.

My mom had the excuse she needed to move. She decided to migrate to another country and left us with our grandmother.

Soon enough, I would learn the truth!

13

Move

Our first move---towards changes

In my sad reality, I saw how our appliances, furniture, and things were being moved to my tia Alma's house.

The apartment was emptying out. What was happening? In less than a week we had moved! All of our belongings were taken to what was going to be our new house (a small space in my aunt's living room.) Luz moved with us. No one said anything or explained to us what was happening.

I don't remember my mom leaving or saying goodbye to us. I recall Luz saying, "I'll take care of you." However, in less than a week our things were gone. My sister was sleeping with my cousin and me. My brother was sleeping with Luz in another room. What happened to our things?

Soon enough, I would learn the truth.

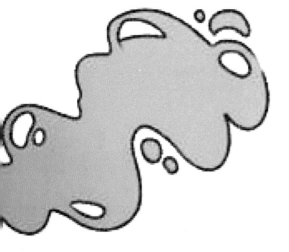

Dark room

Learning to Live---towards the truth

I used to sleep with my cousin, my sister used to sleep with my abuela, and my brother used to sleep with Luz.

The house was big and scary! On the ground level, five steps went up to the sitting room. There were two big living rooms and a small room where my cousin Nicholas used to sleep. The first bedroom was my abuelita's and ours.

The second bedroom was my tio's. The third room was a small one for Luz, her son, and my brother. Then there was a big dark bathroom, we were all afraid to go in. That's why we used to take showers on the patio. The dining room was big enough for two dining tables, and the kitchen had a big charcoal stove.

The patio was in the center of the house and had a double floor where we hid to listen to the adult's conversations. We weren't allowed to sit next to them when they were talking. We didn't stay in that house for too long. From their conversations, we learned that there were too many of us and we needed to move to a bigger house.

Soon enough, I would learn the truth!

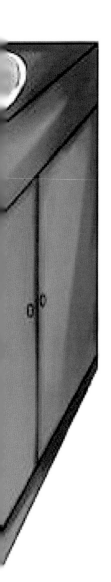

22

Library

Second Move---towards the truth

We moved again, this time to a much bigger house. Double doors marked the entrance and a waiting area with a small library. To the left was a red arch, the entrance to an enormous living room, with a high ceiling and chandeliers.

To the left was my tio's bedroom, which had a balcony. Walking to the right, there was a big bedroom with a double entrance and two double doors connected to another bedroom through a small door. This was our room that we shared with abuelita! Then there was my cousin's room, and the next was my other cousin's bedroom.

There was an empty bedroom followed by an enormous bathroom with plenty of light. Next, there was Luz's bedroom, which wasn't as big as the others. Another bedroom followed and then we had a large dining room big enough for two dining sets. There was a window in between the dining room and the kitchen, and to the left of the kitchen was a small room with ironing boards and different small appliances.

The kitchen was so big it had two different stoves (charcoal and gas) and a small kerosene stove. Next to the kitchen was a patio with a laundry room, plants, and another balcony. My surroundings were looking better. The house was great, but it wasn't mine.

It belonged to my cousins. Everything in my life was changing; we were well taken care of, but our life wasn't the same as I remembered. What happened to life as we knew it? It was gone. We were changed to another school! Had to learn about a new world, had to share a bathroom, a new place at the dinner table, a new time to eat breakfast, a new uniform, and new classmates.

It belonged to my cousins. Everything in my life was changing; we were well taken care of, but our life wasn't the same as I remembered. What happened to life as we knew it? It was gone. We were changed to another school! Had to learn about a new world, had to share a bathroom, a new place at the dinner table, new time to eat breakfast, new uniform, new classmates.

Alady named Esther used to walk us to school and pick us up. No longer was there a blue or red car to take us home. Changes, and more changes. I needed a way to overcome my fear of more changes. I needed a sense of belonging. One day I approached my aunt and asked if I could read the books in the library. She told me specifically to use the short stories encyclopedia.

Right in front of me! Hidden in the library, I found a gold mine, an encyclopedia of short stories. I don't remember how old I was when I learned to read, but reading was my passion. I used to create my own world, and after finishing a short story, I would change the ending to my liking. I created and dreamed of another life, and built my own world. I would come home from school, and

take a book to hide in my bed to read the stories repeatedly.

From then on though, I had to wait for her to come from work so we could talk about my daily reading. My aunt helped me realize that reading skills meant getting to new worlds with your imagination. Those short stories became my new world! I created an imaginative new world where all the changes were mine.

Soon enough, I would learn the truth!

Bats

Third Move---towards the truth!

As time passed by, I learned that my mom would start coming, and going back and forth to the USA. I felt nervous since that meant more changes. However, it made me feel relieved about belonging. Suddenly, one day my mom was back again, and to my surprise, she and Tia Gigi were speaking to each other, and my Tia Gigi's husband was back!!

My playmates and cousins were moving to the south side of the city. We didn't have any more play time! The big house became bigger!!

Still, my cousins would visit occasionally, and we would run from one side of the house to another (it was a long hallway). One day, they came at night, but Abuelita was not there. We started playing, but the hall was too dark. (Abuelita had warned us not to turn the lights on.) But we wanted to play, so we ran back and forth from the dining room to the living room and turned all the lights on.

Suddenly, while I was running, something dropped on my back, but was pulling my hair. I started screaming, and everyone was pointing at my head. I heard a shriek coming from my long hair.

My cousin came at me with a broom. I thought he was going to hit me! Nana Luz came out with a big towel and screamed for everyone to be quiet and for me not to move! She came beside me and pulled my hair so hard that it hurt so much! 'I got it! I got it!' she said.

When I looked at what was inside the towel, I couldn't believe it! When I saw the roof and window rails, I almost fainted. It was a bat! The bats took over all the rails. That was the reason Abuelita told us not to turn the lights on! I begged her to cut my hair. Since then, I've never had long hair.

Soon enough, I would learn the truth!

Movies

My Move---towards the truth

My grandfather on my father's side used to visit us. He used to bring us all the toiletries and leave us money, but we weren't allowed to say hello to my Abuelito Alejo! They would make us hide! I used to hear my Abuelita say that we had gone to visit my tia, Gigi.

I didn't understand Abuelita's reasoning and felt sad and ambivalent about the lies, but she used to say that he was drunk. Every time, after waiting for us, he would cry about missing us and being unable to see us. However, Abuelita would send us to his house for lunch on Sundays. Later, Abuelito would take us to the movies and tell us to invite anyone we liked, so all my cousins would come with us.

Also, he'd tell the workers at the theater to give us anything we wanted, like popcorn, sodas, and candy. He'd also take us to a soda shop where we'd have sandwiches and soda. I had so many questions...but no one would dare ask.

Soon enough, I would learn the truth!

Empty table

Their Move---towards the truth!

Suddenly, my tio Nando was gone. He used to ask us to sit with him at the table (the big dining table). We kids weren't allowed to eat at that table: it was only for grown-ups. He used to say we were the only ones who would make him feel comfortable and welcomed. He would make Luz serve and feed us the same food he was eating, no exceptions! (They used to make him special plates of food.) We liked that, but Abuelita told us not to comment, answer his questions, and say we didn't know anything.

"He's drunk. Don't say a word!" Seeing him looking for someone to talk to was sad, but everyone feared him. I used to tell him that dinner was served and he'd reply "si pero todos ¿dónde están? Tú no me tienes miedo, ven acompañame" His disappearance alarmed us, but they all acted like it was normal. He didn't show up anymore, with men behind him carrying big bags of food. Nor would he invite us to eat out or visit a special place.

Soon enough, I would learn the truth!

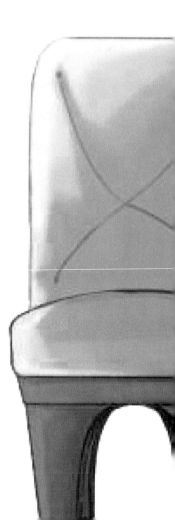

Mountains, beaches

Their move, incognito! ---Towards the truth.

One night, Abuelita said, we are going on a trip, get ready! Luz picked up our stuff, and we were on a bus traveling to Quito in less than an hour. It stopped in a small town, where we used the facilities and ate chicken soup. It was an adventure.

We arrived at around 6 a.m. A taxi was waiting for us. It took us to the south of the city, which was scary. It left us by the corner of a park, but to our surprise, it was the top of a hill, and we had to walk down. My Abuelita knocked at the door several times, but no one answered. Suddenly, an older lady from the next house appeared and told my Abuelita to come in.

To my surprise, tio was there, and he was pleased when he saw us. He told us to get comfortable, and we soon went to the plaza for breakfast. He looked slim and was working in an apothecary. We didn't understand, but we were used to not asking questions and had to make believe nothing was happening. We were happy to see him, but soon enough, we were moving to another city, Ambato, to a beautiful house on top of a hill.

My abuela knew everyone, and to my surprise, Tia Alma arrived soon after. Like always, they asked us to go out and play. We slept there that night. The next day, we packed up everything and were traveling to visit someone in Riobamba. The adventure lasted two weeks. Tio did not return with us. However, we visited him more often. My grandma would take us to the beaches, and the whole family would accompany us. Our life was always a trip. My life became a short story.

Soon enough, I would learn the truth!

USA

A move with dreams and pain--- Life is the truth.

Time passed! One day, my mom said, "OK, it's time to go; we are moving to the United States of America. That's going to be your home!" I was finally going to find out the truth of what my life was supposed to be.

I was starting a new life and had to leave everything behind. What hurt us the most was leaving Luz. She was staying back, but I would keep my promise of not forgetting her.

But life is changing--- Changes that hurt your soul and changes that claim your life.

We made it to the USA with lots of dreams and expectations. The apartment was a tiny one-bedroom. We were finally together as a family. We met new people of different backgrounds. However, things started to get messy because my parents were constantly arguing. My siblings and I tried to ignore their fights, but things escalated to the point that my father would leave and not return for two days. At first, I thought people were very religious. Puerto Ricans have an expression "Ave Maria Purisima," so I would always answer, "sin pecado concebida." They would look at me like I was odd, but no one explained what that meant. We continued learning as days passed by.

Soon enough, I would learn the truth!

Sand

One day, my father was home at night, and we were all sitting in front of the TV. Abruptly, a handful of sand or gravel was thrown at us. My father looked to see if there was a hole in the ceiling. He went around the apartment to look for the culprit, but the apartment was clean, except for the sofa where we were sitting. He called the superintendent and then the Fire Department since he didn't find anything, and the Fire Department couldn't find anything either, but they did witness the sand being thrown.

They told my mom to move since there was enough sand to fill the bathtub. The next day, early in the morning, I heard my mom crying, but I couldn't hear who she was talking to. Suddenly, my sister screamed and said my brother couldn't get up. He was completely covered with sand and complained that his body hurt. I felt cold, and the whole apartment turned into an icebox. We got ready and left the apartment, but my mom said, "I want you to come with me; your siblings are staying with the neighbors."

It was a strange living room, many chairs, red sofa, and shrines full of saints, candles, and different sizes of glasses, goblets of water. I was afraid at first, but it was more of distrust, my mom at first told me to wait outside, but soon she said, "Come in and listen, in case I forget". I was very attentive, but my mind couldn't understand a

word this lady was saying. Soon enough, we left and my mother said we have to pack and find a new place to live. "We have three days."

We visited many apartment buildings until she said, "Thank you, God." Strangely, my mom bought a black hen and took it to a strange lady. My mom used to repeat that everything was going to be fine.

We hadn't seen my father since the day of the sand incident. He got home that night, but to my surprise, my mom had already spoken to the neighbors, and many were also packing. Our neighbors had prepared a bed for us so we wouldn't sleep in that apartment. My father refused to sleep at the neighbor's apartment and stayed behind.

To our surprise, the building superintendent knocked at that apartment for a long time the next day, and there was no answer. My mom told him that my father was there. He called the police, and they wanted to break down the door. My mom had the keys; once they opened the door, they found my father asleep, with his legs and hands tied up. They carried him out of the apartment and told my mom to move out. They couldn't understand what was happening. We moved out that same day.

We moved to a bigger apartment on the sixth floor of a nice building. It was a Friday night, two days after we had moved, when we heard a big explosion. The apartment building we moved out from was on fire! Thankfully, many of our neighbors had moved out.

Soon enough, I would learn the truth!

High School

Movements of the spirits! ---Towards the truth

My mom and dad took me to a big building. They said it would change my way of looking at life. Education was the only way to succeed, and that was the place. I was so happy; my aunt always said learning would be the only thing no one could take away from me. The school gave me an exam to place me in the correct grade. I knew enough high school subjects, but my social and emotional skills were not mature enough to survive in that new world. I was attending High School, but I was only 13 years old!

The next day, I was placed in room 413. They gave me a schedule to follow, which I didn't understand. I sat the whole day in the same place. No one asked me anything; I figured my name must be there since they were always looking at a red book. It was chaos! I didn't understand anything the teachers were saying! I was so afraid! A week later, a teacher approached me, but I didn't understand a word she said. Finally, she had a student translate for her.

The girl said the teacher was surprised that all my classes were in the same room. She asked me if I knew my class schedule, and I said, "I don't understand it." She told me I was supposed to look for the room numbers for my classes. When the bell rang, I left to look for my new class, but couldn't find it! I got lost! There were so many

people coming and going. I went from one side of the school to another without seeing it. I left the school in desperation, pain, and anxiety, but when I turned around and looked at my surroundings, I knew I was lost. Everything looked the same. I asked a lady in Spanish about getting home, and she told me to take a bus. I got on the bus but didn't know which one was my stop. I got off the bus too early and walked and walked until I found a bank I'd seen before while walking with my mom.

To my surprise, the lady that always helped my mom was not there. I found out that all the banks looked the same, but the guard was very helpful and asked me in Spanish for my address and told me which way to go to get to the branch close to where I lived. Finally, after hours of walking, I got to the street where my apartment building was. My heart felt like I was collapsing, but sure enough I found my building and made it home.

When my mother asked me about my day, I lied telling her everything went smoothly. The next day, instead of going to school, I went upstairs to the building's roof, found an old chair and started to read a book my mom bought me. I went upstairs for almost a week, until the school called my mom to tell her I hadn't been attending my classes. My mom went crazy, but I told her I didn't want to go.

The next day, she went to school with me and stayed with me the whole day. She continued taking me to school, but I would wait for her to leave and then leave the school. One day a security guard followed me, so I made him believe I had a class downstairs.

That is when I found out that there was a Spanish auto mechanics class in the school's sub-basement, and that caught my attention. I understood everything they were saying and felt comfortable. The school called my mom again, saying that I was cutting classes. My mom came to school and got me a counselor.

Finally, I told someone that no one told me classes were on different floors and that the first number on the door number meant the floor. I loved the auto mechanic class because I understood what they were saying. The advisor let me continue attending that class. However, I still felt hopeless and without a purpose for continuing there.

The counselor asked a student to attend classes with me because she spoke Spanish. As luck would have it, I didn't understand her Spanish. I was baffled. One day, the Math teacher asked me, "Did you bring your homework?" She translated saying, "Trajiste la tarea?" To me, 'la tarea' meant house chores, so I said no; how would I bring the broom, mop, etc? Everyone laughed at me! I cried, feeling stupid!

That's when the teacher realized I was not from the Caribbean and my language was Spanish, but my idiomatic expressions and idiosyncrasies were different.

The next day, my history and geography teacher gave me a test to take and decided that I didn't belong there because I was too advanced, but I begged him to let me stay because I felt welcome in that class. He allowed me to stay, but I had to go earlier everyday to take English Language classes.

My life was turning around. He also advised me to take a photographic memory test. To my shock, he told me, "You are full of surprises," and "You have a photographic memory." He said that we needed to work on that. Finally, I felt like I was accomplishing things at school. The school was becoming my life.

Soon enough, I would learn the truth!

58

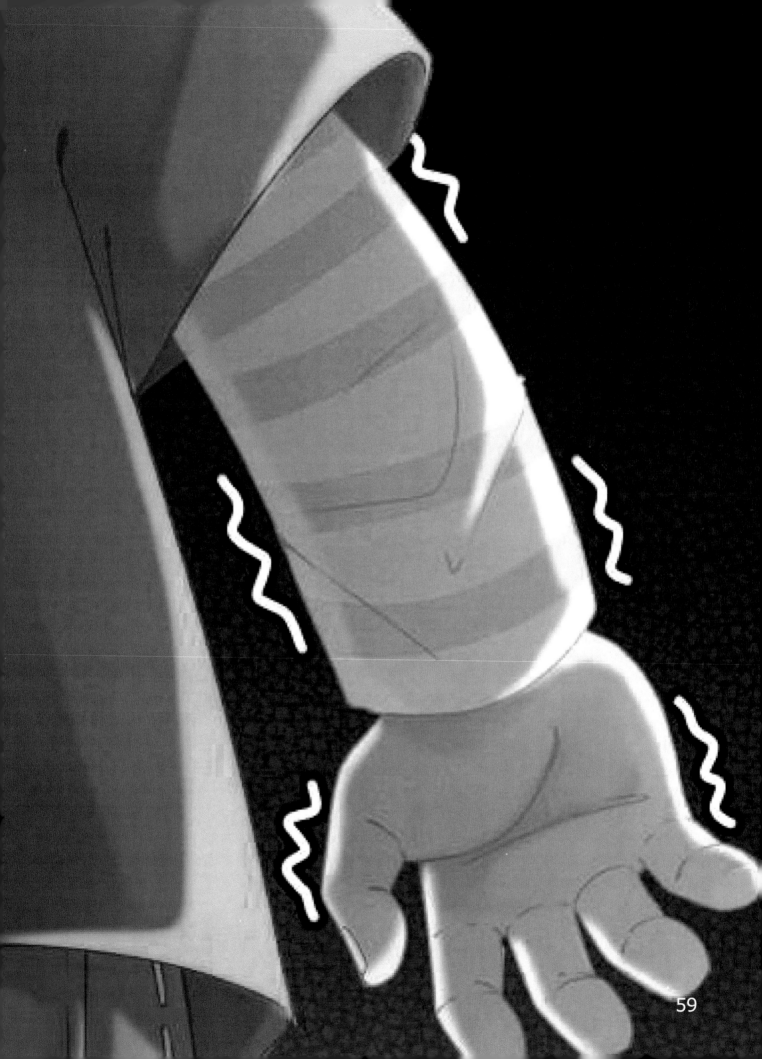

Shivers

Wrong move---towards our reality

I don't understand what happened, but my mother told us we were moving again to a first-floor apartment. I felt a cold breeze in my arms, remembering something the strange lady had said, "Always try to live in an apartment on the third floor or above. Don't move to a lower floor, or your husband will leave you. He'll disappear." It seems my mother had forgotten about the warning. I was afraid! We moved again. Everything went smoothly for the next couple of months, but the apartment had tension and a heavy atmosphere. My mom was no longer calm. She was always stressed out.

Soon enough, I would learn the truth!

People waiting for a cab

Movement to the past---movement towards the truth

One day, my mother said, "We are returning to visit. It's just a family vacation.". We traveled back and had a great time with the family. We had time to play with our cousins and visit everyone. My grandfather gave my mom money for a down payment for a house. We were returning from that trip with a dream of buying a house.

After going through U.S. customs, my father suddenly said, "Get all the bags; I'm going to get the car." He had left the car parked at the airport. My father left us stranded in an airport with no place to go. We waited hours for him, but he never came back.

Soon enough, I would learn the truth!

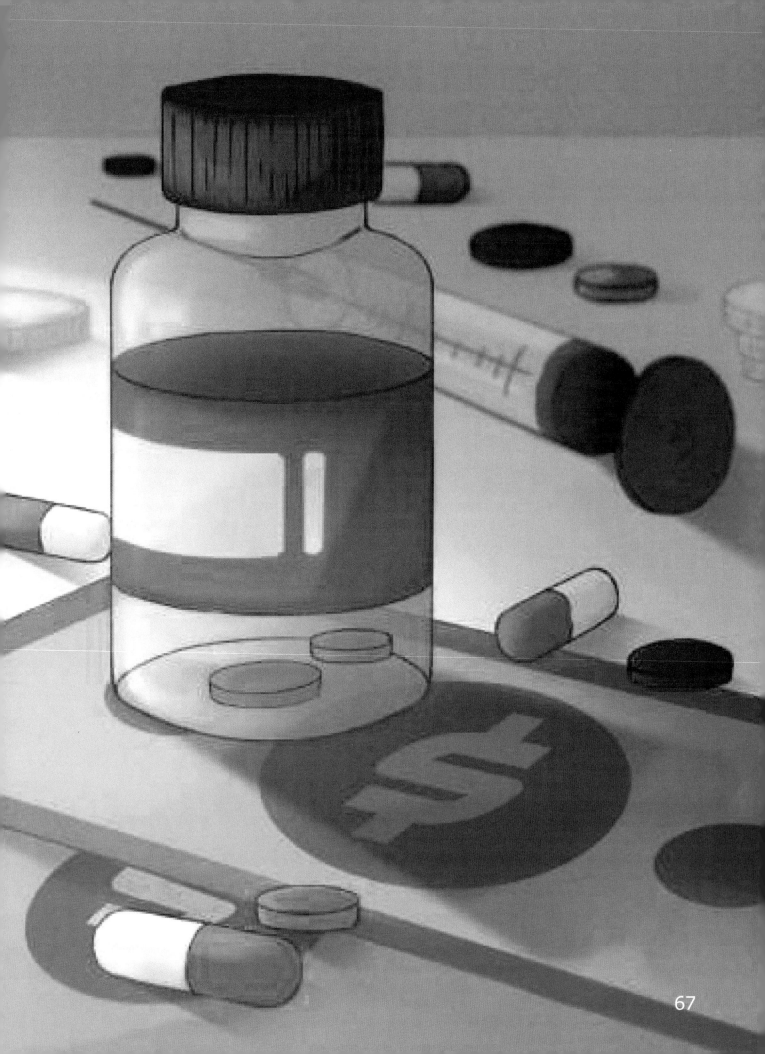

Money, drugs

Moving to our destiny---towards the truth!

Thankfully my sister's friend spoke to her mom and she took us in until my mom found a place to live. We moved to a fourth-floor apartment. The neighbors next door used to sell drugs. However, we had a place to sleep, a place to call home. We didn't see my father for six months; he came back once when he brought our dog back.

Then, he would come and give us twenty dollars, but every time I went to get the money, he would talk about my mom, and I had to hear him cursing her. I used to cry so much until one day; my mom told him to stop abusing me and never come back. We didn't need his money.

We had to learn to survive with one or two dollars a week to eat. My mother would give me a dollar for a bag of chicken hearts or gizzards and another for pasta or rice. We ate and survived! My mother faced our new life with courage and determination. On the other hand, I had to face changes again and became hesitant, indecisive, and lacking self-esteem.

I was an angry soul with too many questions that no one could answer. As time passed, I started looking for somewhere to belong, turning to different religions for answers. I joined the Evangelists, Adventists, Mormons, and other denominations. Why did we have to come to this country? What happened to my beautiful family? Why? Why?

Life had many surprises for us. Mom worked day and night as a seamstress. Months later, she won a lottery, and we moved out of that place, bought furniture, and finally had our own rooms. Our life got better day by day. Mom worked and worked! We used to help her at home; we learned to sew and became seamstresses so that she could sleep a bit more.

I graduated from high school. I needed to find work fast to help my mom, so I went to a business school and became an Executive/ Bilingual Secretary. I worked and worked, but I felt unsatisfied and used to cry every night. One day, my mom asked me directly, what was wrong with me? All I said was, "I am not a secretary! I want more." She said, "OK, do you want to attend college?" I immediately said, "YES!" So I did! I applied and was accepted.

Soon enough, I would learn the truth!

Religions

My move---towards my life!

One of my first classes in college had to do with the similarities and differences between religions. During that time, I had stopped attending services and masses and felt angry with God. I took this class to inform everyone that everything based on religion was false. I created a questionnaire that showed the hypocrisy of all the priests, pastors, etc.

The truth was that I needed to talk to someone about my feelings. After weeks of research, I went to a Catholic Church and asked for a priest. I wondered why God wants us to suffer, to feel hate. Why did we have to come to the States to lose our family?

I tried to open those big wooden doors of the church, but they were so heavy. I got so angry. I thought God didn't want to hear me. I went to the parish office to ask why the doors were locked. Isn't there an open-door policy? The girl told me to wait and that a priest would talk to me.

The first words that came out of my mouth were, "WHY? Don't lie to me," I said, the church doors were locked, and I couldn't open them. He responded, "The doors are open; follow me." He asked me to try to open them again, and surprisingly, they opened without any problem. I started crying!
After speaking to him for a while, I understood that my

frustration, anger, and necessity to blame others for my pain weren't allowing me to see the real culprit.

Since the beginning, I had blamed myself, thinking everything we had gone through was my fault. When my mother left us to follow my father, I thought it was because we weren't good enough for her.

When she brought us with them so that we could become a real family, it was just a mirage of lies. The education that would change our lives and give us the opportunities to excel wasn't for me. All the frustration, work, and necessities we had gone through were pain to make us pay for what?

I was ready to learn the truth!

Without a plan

One of my favorite hiding places was the movie theater. Many might say, 'What a fool, how can you take that from a romantic comedy?' It was my life with a different perspective, and I needed to believe everything would change. My life had turned upside down. I needed to learn not to trust the first impression! I thought you must go through ups and downs to get where you need to be.

It's strange, but a movie changed my thinking because I decided to follow its subliminal message.

It was based on the life of a librarian who had terrible experiences. Her life was in despair; as the movie's song said, "She lived in a shell, was doing ok, but not very well."

No one understood her troubles; she couldn't express her daily life, emotions, and fears. Not even she could understand what she was going through. Many thought she was a fool, a crazy woman who didn't know what was happening. That was me. I needed to trust again, believe in people, and retake a chance. I had to learn to have faith in people and God again.

Going for my truth!

Family

Opening my eyes---towards the truth

Before pursuing my dream, I had to learn the truth about my insecurities and why they existed. I approached my mom and asked her a simple question. WHY? She couldn't answer, but I would do it for her: it was for love.

So much LOVE for a man that she didn't know how to handle it. She thought that caring, moving from one place to another, would make him change. She felt that having the whole family together would keep him from leaving. One person's love isn't enough to support a FAMILY.

Family is based on a support system where all members work towards a dream, which later becomes a reality. My absolute truth relies on my experiences and the lives of many who have faced the same realities. The truth is, those experiences made me who I am.

81

My own survival Kit

Social Work, or Psychology. My love for reading and changing the ending of the novels was my calling. One day, after a Literature class, while waiting for my next class, some classmates approached me and asked me to review the lesson we had just finished.

I said, of course, and went over the main points and told them what I thought the Professor expected from us. At one point, I just looked at them and asked what they thought was my strongest subject. They just smiled at me and said, "You're a teacher! You're a real professor! Haven't you noticed we always stay behind to ask you to go over the lessons?"

Was it reality or just a dream?

AuthorHouse™
1663 Liberty Drive
Bloomington, IN 47403
www.authorhouse.com
Phone: 833-262-8899

Because of the dynamic nature of the Internet, any web addresses or links contained in this book may have changed since publication and may no longer be valid. The views expressed in this work are solely those of the author and do not necessarily reflect the views of the publisher, and the publisher hereby disclaims any responsibility for them.

Any people depicted in stock imagery provided by Getty Images are models, and such images are being used for illustrative purposes only.
Certain stock imagery © Getty Images.

This book is printed on acid-free paper.

ISBN: 979-8-8230-1822-7 (sc)
ISBN: 979-8-8230-1823-4 (hc)
ISBN: 979-8-8230-1824-1 (e)

Library of Congress Control Number: 2023922492

Print information available on the last page.

Published by AuthorHouse 04/16/2024

authorHOUSE®

Printed in the United States
by Baker & Taylor Publisher Services